LEON
AND THE
LAMB

JOAN E. FRANCES

To order additional copies of this book, contact:
Xlibris
844-714-8691
www.Xlibris.com
Orders@Xlibris.com

ISBN: Softcover   978-1-6698-6281-9
         Hardcover   978-1-6698-6282-6
         EBook   978-1-6698-6280-2
Library of Congress Control Number: 2023900898
Print information available on the last page

Rev. date: 01/17/2023

Prologue

Children, listen when I say
There will be a future day
When the lion and the lamb
Will be friends...
They will frolic and play as one
And nap side by side
In the afternoon sun

And this is their story

Joan E. Frances

Dedication Page

I would like to thank the people who have been supportive for this book project.

To my family, my husband Daniel who was supportive of my efforts. To my son, Peter who was my editor and my other son, Gregory who was the catalyst in rekindling my love for writing.

Also, Thank you for the Xlibris illustrations team for the fine work they have done with the illustrations.

Leon and the Lamb

Leon, the lion, woke up. He uncurled himself and stretched. He opened his mouth to ROAR, but instead he sneezed. He sneezed so hard the cover from his mattress and pillow burst and feathers filled his room.

Leon flicked his tail unrolling a big red handkerchief. He blew his nose, and tears rolled from his red watery eyes.

"I should be waking up with a ROAR!" he cried and brushed at the feathers fluttering around him.

"I was told I am 'King' of the Jungle' and also 'King of the farms and mountainside too.' Here I am sniffling and snuffling. "What oh what, am I going to do?"

"I was asked to keep everyone safe by roaring so our community would know my roar would frighten away bad people and nasty wild animals."

His desperate words were interrupted with another sneeze, "How can I do that if I can't roar and let everyone know I am here protecting them from harm?"

What would it take to solve his problem? Leon did not know.

Leon opened his dresser drawer and took out two big red handkerchiefs. One he folded and tucked into his jeans pocket. The other he folded and tied around his tail. Leon always took an extra handkerchief because of his sneezing problem.

His mother called, "Leon, come down. Your breakfast is ready."

He walked down the stairs, gave his mother a kiss, and sat down to breakfast. She informed him, "I called Dr. Mason and told him about your problem. He said he could see you this morning. Stop at his office." She added, "Doctors know how to solve problems."

"Yes mother, I will." he answered and sneezed once more.

When Leon sat down at the table he noticed an envelope lying next to his plate. His mother pointed to it and said, "The envelope was in today's mailbox and it is addressed to you." It's from The Committee for Residential Safety." Leon pulled the letter from the envelope and read it out loud.

Dear Leon,

It has come to the attention of our council members that we have not heard you roar. The job requires you to roar first thing in the morning, and also at bedtime. If we do not hear from you in the next two days, we will have to find a replacement for your job. Our citizens have to know we are looking out for their safety. We have several residents interested in your job. You were our first choice. This request is urgent and we need to hear from you.

Sincerely,
Clyde H. Pepperton, Council President

Leon's mother asked, "Who do you think would be better suited for the safety job." Leon put down his glass of milk and said, "Before the council hired me, they had talked to the Giraffe family. Because the giraffe has such a long neck, he can look over the countryside and see if there is something wrong and report it to the local safety team. Another is the Zebra family. They would like the job because they can run very fast and catch anyone who is a threat to our homes."

I was given the job because my roaring frightens bad people and nasty animals and they quickly run away from here and don't return."

6

After breakfast and after helping his mother with the morning clean up, he said "Goodbye mother. I will return this afternoon and let you know what the doctor recommends."

He sneezed two times before walking out the door.

Leon stepped into Doctor Mason's office. "Good morning Leon."

"Your mother called and said you have a problem. She said you wake up every morning sneezing instead of roaring." You need to roar so everyone will know you are there to protect them. Is that correct?"

"Yes, that is true," replied Leon. This time he sneezed so hard the window shade flew up and flapped around the roller. The doctor looked at the shade. He scratched his chin. "Hmm" he mumbled. I can see this problem is going to be difficult to solve."

"Leon, hop up on the table and let's have a look at you."
Dr. Mason listened to Leon's heart. He looked in Leon's
ears. He peered at Leon's red watery eyes. "Hmm" the
doctor repeated and scratched his chin again. "Open your
mouth wide. I want to look down your throat"

The doctor depressed Leon's tongue. "Say A-h-h." Leon
opened his mouth wide and said "ahh, ahh, AHHCHOO! He
sneezed so hard the doctor's glasses slid down his nose.
The doctor adjusted his glasses and brushed a stray feather
from Leon's jeans. "Do you sleep on a feather mattress?"

"Yes" doctor." Leon sneezed. "A feather mattress and a
feather pillow too."

"Hmm." the doctor said for the third time and walked to
his desk.

"Leon I think I might have an answer to your problem." He took paper and pencil and started writing.

"The feathers from your mattress and pillow tickle your nose. That is why you sneeze". He tore the paper from the pad and handed it to Leon.

The paper read:

DOCTOR'S ORDERS
I hereby order one lamb's wool blanket and pillow from the Countryside Sheep and Lambskin Shoppe for my patient Leon. He also needs to replace his feather mattress.
Signed: Dr. Thomas Mason Official Title

"Leon if you get these items, tomorrow you will wake up roaring instead of sneezing".

The doctor smiled. He was pleased with himself. He believed he had solved a problem.

Leon left the doctor's office deep in thought. He did not feel, in spite of what Dr. Mason had said, that his problem would be easy to solve. Besides his medical problem with his sneezing instead of roaring, the barnyard sheep were afraid of him. He looked at the doctor's order and shook his head.

"After all, I am still a lion even though I go around sneezing instead of roaring". Then he had a thought, I'll go to my favorite 'thinking spot' and see if I can find a way to solve my problem.

He put the doctor's order in his pocket and started up the steep winding path to the top of the hill. He walked over to his favorite rock and was ready to sit down when he heard a small voice calling,

"Help! help!

Leon looked around. There was no one on the hill. Again he heard that small voice calling out. Carefully he walked to the edge of the cliff and lowered himself to the ground. He looked over the edge to see who was calling for help.

Leon gasped!

Below him was a little lamb clinging to a very thin tree branch. The branch was about to snap sending the lamb tumbling down the steep stony hillside where it would be scraped and cut by jagged stones. Leon could see the lamb needed help quickly before that branch snapped.

Leon pulled himself up and looked around. He shouted, "Hold on, I'll find a big stick for you to grab and I'll pull you up."

He looked around for a sturdy stick. There was no stick on the hillside.

"What am I going to do?' Another sneeze interrupted his desperate words. He took out his red handkerchief and quickly blew his nose.

Suddenly the answer came to him. He would unroll the handkerchief which he had tied to his tail and tell the lamb to grab it and he would pull the lamb to safety.

He shouted to the lamb, "There is no sturdy stick up here but I have tied a big red handkerchief to my tail for you to grab".

He unrolled the handkerchief, sat down as close as possible to the edge of the cliff and flicked his tail, over the side.

"When I say 'One", grab the handkerchief and hang on. The lamb tried to grab the red handkerchief dangling from Leon's tail, but he was not directly below the lamb. The lamb called out," I can't reach the handkerchief."

Leon rolled over and looked down. Once more he got up and walked to a jagged edge of the cliff, lowered himself to make sure the lamb would be directly below him. He sat down closer to the edge and flicked his tail, and shouted "When I say one, grab the handkerchief."

Before the lamb could grab the handkerchief, the tree branch tore a little. Also the place where Leon was sitting was not sturdy and stones were starting to roll down the cliff.

"One" Leon shouted. This time the lamb was able to grab the big red handkerchief just as the branch tore away from the hillside.

"I caught the handkerchief." the lamb called out.

Leon stood up. "When I count two, I'll start pulling you up". He called back. The lamb's rescue was underway. "Two" Leon counted before he sneezed. The lamb started scrambling up the steep hillside. The tiny tree was now tumbling down the hillside, followed by many sharp stones and loose dirt. "Three", Leon counted and the lamb was on top of the hill.

Leon said, "You are safe now" and sneezed again.

The tiny lamb looked at Leon and said "You are a lion." She started backing away from Leon as tears rolled down her cheeks. "Are you going to hurt me?" she asked "The barnyard sheep are afraid of you. The lamb continued, I was told to stay away from big animals but you saved my life. Why did you do that?" The lamb asked.

Leon answered, "I am not going to hurt you. I saved you because that is part of my job. I did not want to see you tumble down that hill where you would have been hurt from the sharp jagged stones and loose dirt."

"Why were you up here? Leon inquired.

The lamb answered, "I wanted to see what the barnyard looked like from the top of the hill, but I walked too close to the edge and stumbled. I fell over the cliff. The only thing I could grab was that thin tree branch."

The little lamb looked up at Leon and said "That was a brave thing you did. You could have tumbled down the hillside too." Look over there where you were sitting. There is a big gap."

Now that the lamb was no longer afraid of Leon she asked, "What is your name?"

"My name is Leon." he smiled shyly. "I'm the one who is supposed to roar in the morning and evening to let the countryside know I am keeping them safe, but I sneeze instead of roaring and I don't know how to solve my problem."

"I'm going to call you Leon", the lamb answered. "Now I remember my mother, and the other sheep, talking about you." The lamb yawned. "They said they were afraid of you because you were a lion."

Leon asked, "What is your name?" The lamb answered, "My name is Lucy".

Leon was about to tell Lucy more about his job and why they should not be afraid of him, when he noticed how tired she was. "Would you like me to take you home"? He asked"?" Lucy nodded. "OK".

Leon gently picked Lucy up, put her on his back. She was so tired she fell asleep as he wrapped his paws around hers which were over his shoulders. Together they started down the steep hill toward the barnyard.

As Leon and Lucy came closer to the barnyard, he could see some of the sheep having a picnic lunch in the nearby pasture. They spotted him and grabbed their picnic baskets and ran to find the lamb's mother. One of the sheep shouted, "A lion is in the pasture and he is carrying your baby on his back!" Then they ran to their stalls inside the barn. Now they felt safe. Two of the sheep went to a window to see what would happen.

The lamb's mother grabbed an iron poker from her fireplace and started running toward Leon and her little lamb.

They saw her shouting. "Put my baby down on the ground. You big nasty lion. Do you hear me?"

She walked to where Leon was standing and waved the iron poker at him. He stopped.

"Yes ma'am I hear you." He managed to say before he had to sneeze. He sneezed so loud it woke the lamb. Lucy saw his mother waving the iron poker at Leon.

"Mother, stop!" she cried. "This lion is my friend, Leon. He saved my life! Put that iron poker down and I will tell you what happened to me". Leon reached up and gently removed Lucy from his back and set her on the ground.

The lamb's mother looked as though she didn't see how a lion could save her little baby. She asked "So how did this big nasty lion save my little baby's life?" She stopped waving the poker at Leon. Instead she said, "I'm listening."

Then Lucy told her mother about how brave Leon had been. She told her mother why she had climbed up the steep hill. How she walked to the edge, stumbled, and fell over the side. "All I could grab was a thin tree branch" she continued, "The thin tree branch I was holding onto was about to tear and tumble down the rocky hillside where I would have been cut by loose stones rolling down the hillside. I called "Help! Leon heard me.""

Then Lucy looked up at Leon. She put one of her paws in Leon's and said, "Leon could have tumbled down the hillside with me because he had to sit down where stones and loose dirt were running down the hillside. He too would have tumbled down and been badly cut by the jagged stones before I could grab his tail with the big red handkerchief tied to it. He pulled me to safety, mom."

Lucy's mother lowered the iron poker. "I'm sorry I yelled at you and for waving this iron poker in your face. This morning when I woke up, I could not find my baby. The barnyard sheep helped me look for her, but she was no where to be found. I thought some nasty animal had taken her."

She looked at her baby, and in a stern voice said, "Don't you ever sneak off like that again!" Lucy looked at Leon and her mother. "I promise never to go anywhere by myself unless you, mom, or Leon is with me." Lucy squeezed Leon's paw. "I really learned a valuable lesson today." Leon nodded and sneezed once more.

That was a brave thing you did for my baby." Lucy's mother said. That hillside is dangerous and none of the sheep ever climb up to the top." She laid the fireplace poker on the ground. "Is there something I can do to repay you?" she asked

Now Leon saw the solution to his sneezing problem. He pulled the doctor's order from his pocket. He handed it to the lamb's mother. "Can you fill this for me?" He asked

She smiled as she read the doctor's order. Leon said "I need the blanket and pillow so I will stop sneezing. He sneezed and looked at the ground. "I also need a new mattress that isn't filled with feathers. Do you know where I can get one?"

Leon continued, "Don't be afraid when you hear me roar. I was hired to protect you and everyone who lives here and also those who live in the jungle, the mountainside, the village, and the farms." Leon sneezed again. "I was hired to protect you and bad people who might be trying to hurt you and also nasty animals who want to do the same." He sneezed once more and looked shyly at Lucy and her mother.

"When I stop sneezing and find a way to roar, the bad people and nasty animals are so frightened they run away and do not return." That is why I was hired by The Safety Council." Leon explained.

The lamb's mother said, "Now I understand why we should not be afraid and if we have any of these problems, we will let you know."

She continued, "I can fill your doctor's order so you will stop sneezing. She walked to her shop. Opened a large trunk and pulled out two beautiful lamb's wool blankets. She went into the backroom and brought out two lamb's wool pillows.

"Leon, she said, "One of these blankets you should throw over your mattress. That will protect you from the feathers. "The other one will keep you warm when the weather is cold."

"Leon, you are a very special lion and these gifts are a thank you for saving my baby." She said as she folded the blankets and put them in a brightly colored bag and handed them to Leon. She found another pretty bag and put the two pillows in it.

Leon said' I am very happy I saved your little baby and now I want to go home and tell my mother what happened this afternoon"

Leon turned to his new friend, "Would you like to go on a picnic tomorrow"? He asked

Lucy answered, "Can we go up that steep hill so I can see what the barnyard and pasture look like from there?"

Leon smiled before he sneezed and nodded "Yes". "We will set up our picnic basket and sun umbrella under the big tree on that same hill. You will be able to see the entire countryside. It is nice and sunny there. When we feel tired, we can nap in the shade of the big tree on the hill".

That evening he took out the big blanket, and placed it over his mattress. He also put the two lamb's wool pillows on his bed and went to sleep.

Leon woke early the next day. He uncurled himself and stretched. He opened his mouth and ROARED! That roar was heard throughout the jungle, the forest, the farms, and the village and up and down the mountainside.

He walked to his dresser and took out all his big red handkerchiefs, folded them and put them in a box. He walked down the stairs to the kitchen.

His mother was smiling and said, "I heard that roar. From now on you will not be sneezing anymore." Leon kissed his mother's cheek and handed her the box.

"Would you put these big red handkerchiefs away? I won't need them anymore" His mother smiled and said, "Gladly, Leon."

After breakfast Leon told his mother that he and his new friend, Lucy, they were going on a picnic. "Would you pack a picnic lunch for Lucy and me?" he asked. His mother replied, "I will be happy to do that. I am so happy your problem is solved and now you can keep your job."

When he arrived at the barnyard Lucy was waiting. He picked her up, along with the picnic blanket, the picnic basket, and a sun umbrella. He handed Lucy a pair of sun glasses which matched the ones Leon was wearing.

Together they started on their journey toward the steep hill. .

All morning, Leon pointed to the special places he protected. He showed Lucy where his house was and how it looked from the top of the hill. He pointed to her house too. After their picnic lunch they were both tired and Leon asked, "Do you mind if I roar once more before we take a short nap?"

The sleepy Lucy shook her head nodding "No, I won't mind." she answered.

Leon opened his mouth. Then he closed it. His friend was asleep and he did not want to wake her. He thought to himself, I can roar later or any time I want to. Instead he curled his tail around his new friend and together they fell asleep in the shade of their favorite tree.

Epilogue

Wording from the Book of Isaiah - Chapter 11: Verse 6
The lion will lie down with the goat...
and a little child will lead them.
I needed to change the Bible verse from goat to
lamb because my story is about a lion and a lamb.
I really believe Isaiah will understand
why I had to make the change.

Printed in the United States
by Baker & Taylor Publisher Services